Hotwife Party Kitten

Shared With His Coworkers

Lacey Cross

TWISTED ROSE
· PUBLISHING ·

CONTENTS

CHAPTER 1

I'm in the bedroom searching for holes in my fishnet stockings. These babies are crucial for my costume, so I'm making sure I don't need to buy new ones before my husband's work Halloween party. The bedroom door creaks open, and when Lucas walks in, he drops his work bag on the bed with a sigh.

"Baby, I've got some bad news."

I glance up from my stockings, and my heart does a little flip-flop. Uh-oh. "What's up, love?"

"Work needs me to fly out to the other office for a couple of days to meet with a new client," he explains, running a hand through his hair.

My brain short-circuits for a second. Travel? That's new. And right before Halloween? Crap.

"But what about the party?" I can hear the pout in my tone, but I don't care. Disappointment and irritation war inside me. There goes my plan to strut around as a sexy cat and get frisky with my husband.

Lucas pulls me into a hug. "I know, and I'm sorry. But I want you to go without me," he says, his voice dropping into that suggestive tone that never fails to make my toes curl.

My body snaps to attention, and I quirk an eyebrow. "Really? You want me to go to your work party alone?"

"Well, not entirely alone." He gives me a mischievous grin, and slides his hands down to cup my ass. "I might arrange for someone to entertain you."

A laugh bubbles up from my chest. "You're incorrigible, you know that?"

He brushes his lips against my ear, making me tremble. "And you love it. Besides, we both know you want me to find a guy to fuck you hard."

His words send a jolt of electricity straight to my core. God, he's right. I do. As his lips meet mine, I can feel Ms. Kitty—the name I jokingly call my pussy—growing damp. Maybe this Halloween won't be such a bust after all.

The next two days are torture. Lucas is gone, and my mind is a constant whirlwind of fantasies about the mystery man he's arranged for me. All he told me was that I'd know when the guy talked to me. Cryptic bastard.

I try to distract myself by working on my latest erotic vampire novel, but it's no use. My characters keep morphing into potential candidates for my upcoming adventure. As an indie author, I usually love losing myself in my steamy stories, but right now, reality is way more exciting than fiction.

It feels weird to think about walking into his work party alone, but I've met enough of his coworkers over the years. Still, it's a big company. I try not to obsess over which of them might end up balls-deep inside me by the end of the night. The surprise is half the fun, and Lucas knows me better than I know myself sometimes. I trust him to pick the perfect guy.

Finally, it's Halloween night. I'm standing in front of the full-length mirror, fussing with the tail on my cat costume for the millionth time. The black dress hugs every curve of my petite 5'1" frame, making my generous breasts look even more tempting. I feel sexy as hell. A pair of cat ears nestled in my long blonde hair, some whiskers drawn with eyeliner, and a choker with a little bell complete the look.

I slide on my black fishnet thigh high stockings, loving how they make my legs look long and irresistible despite my short stature. The silicone lace band at the top grips my thighs, holding them securely in place without the need for a garter belt. They're the perfect finishing touch, adding just the right amount of naughty to my costume.

When I slip on my black heels, I instantly feel more powerful. The extra height changes my posture, making me walk with more purpose. As I move, the bell on my choker jingles softly. I can't help but imagine the sound it'll make as I ride some stranger later, chiming with each thrust. The thought makes me flush, and my pussy buzzes with anticipation.

God, I hope Lucas found someone with a big cock. I want to feel stretched, filled, used in the most delicious way possible. Just thinking about a thick shaft sliding into me makes me clench my thighs together. Ms. Kitty is definitely complaining about the lack of action lately. Yeah, Lucas has been swamped with work, but I know better than to take matters into my own hands now. I want to be on edge and ready for whatever—or whomever—the night brings.

I add a final touch of red lipstick and admire the full effect. My heart races with anticipation. This isn't just another boring work party. It's a chance for something wild.

One last glance in the mirror, tousling my blonde hair for that perfect look, before grabbing my purse to put my phone in, and I'm out the door. The night is full of possibilities, and I can't wait to see where it takes me—or who it leads me to. Ms. Kitty is ready for action, and so am I.

CHAPTER 2

My stilettos click against the marble, each step energizing me. God, I'm nervous. Excited. Both. I pause just inside the ballroom, taking in the decor. Holy hell, Lucas's work really outdid themselves renting this place.

The air's thick with excitement and expensive perfumes. It's adults-only tonight, and boy, does it show. Dim lights, velvet nooks, plush furniture just begging to be touched—it's decadent. My writer's brain is on overdrive, filing away details for a future story. This place is pure inspiration.

I glide deeper into the crowd, anticipation coiling low in my belly. What's my darling husband cooked up this time? Knowing Lucas, it's bound to be delightfully naughty. The thought sends electricity crackling through me. Ms. Kitty stirs, already interested. God, I'm living for this—the sheer adventure of it all. This is why I love our lifestyle.

My eyes dart from face to face, searching for that spark. Lucas promised I'd know the guy when I saw him. But who? A vampire in a cape brushes past, his fangs gleaming. I smirk, thinking of my latest reverse harem novel. My dress hugs every curve, leaving just enough to tease. I can feel the weight of people staring as I sashay to the bar, dodging a playful fairy and her pirate companion. Time to quench my thirst and start the hunt.

I flash the bartender, dressed as a prohibition-era gangster, my sexiest smile. "Sparkling water, please. Any flavor is fine."

The bartender tries to avoid staring at my cleavage as he hands me my drink. He should just look. This dress makes these girls look spectacular tonight. I take a sip, and the strawberry bubbles fizz on my tongue as I turn to survey my hunting grounds. Game on.

That's when I spot him. Martin. Lucas's coworker. He's tall, broad-shouldered, and has a jawline that could cut glass. He's dressed as a gladiator, all bronzed skin and rippling muscles. When he cuts a path in my direction, a shiver runs through me. Oh, hello there. Somehow, I just know Lucas chose him for me. God, I love my husband.

"Hello, Martin," I purr as he approaches.

His voice rumbles so deep I swear I feel it in my chest. "Good evening. Is the sexy kitten looking to play with a gladiator tonight?"

Ms. Kitty perks up, very interested and embarrassingly wet. I arch an eyebrow. "Maybe...it depends on what you're offering." I take another sip, trying to play it cool. "You know, I'm not just any kitten. I have...particular tastes."

He leans in close, his growl making my toes curl. "And what makes you think I can't satisfy those tastes?"

Oh, honey. You have no idea what you're in for. I smile and channel my inner seductress. "Well...I'm not easily impressed. You'll need more than a good line." I step closer, almost pressing against him. The charge between us makes my skin tingle. "Tell me something...intriguing. Something that makes me want to get to know you more."

He doesn't back down. Instead, his lips brush my ear, and my pussy clenches with need. "How about this? Your husband rented a suite for us upstairs, away from the noise and the crowd. A place where we can explore those particular tastes of yours."

Holy hell, Lucas got us a room? My body's practically humming with excitement. But I'm not ready to give in just yet. This is too much fun. "Tempting. But what makes you think I'm interested in exploring anything with you?"

He smirks. "Because, I can see it in your eyes. The hunger, the desire. You want this as much as I do." His finger traces a line down my arm, leaving goosebumps in its wake. "And I've been told I'm quite talented with my tongue. You could always rate me afterwards."

Oh god, he better be fabulous with that tongue, or I might actually give him a 5 out of 10. I've got some pretty high standards these days. My body's on fire, every nerve ending screaming for his touch. I flash him a 'come hither' smile. "All right, let's see what you've got. But fair warning: I'm not just any kitten. I'm the kind that bites."

He laughs, "I'll remember that," as I down the rest of my drink, set the glass on the bar, and grab my purse. I take Martin's hand, feeling the warmth of his skin against mine. "Lead the way."

My heart pounds as we weave through the crowd. The elevator ride is a blur of anticipation and heated glances. As soon as his suite door closes behind us, Martin is on me. His hands grip my waist, the leather of his costume creaking as he pulls me against him, his lips claiming mine in a fierce kiss.

Our tongues swirl together, and I feel light headed. Before I lose myself fully, I pull out of his arms and tease, "Not so fast, champ. You promised me a demonstration of your skills, remember?"

I guide him towards the king-sized bed, pushing him down so he's sitting on the edge. I stand between his legs, my hands resting on his shoulders, feeling the faux leather under my fingers.

He looks up at me, a wicked grin spreading across his face. "Oh, I remember. And I always deliver on my promises."

His hands slide up my thighs, the rough texture of my fishnet stockings adding an extra layer of sensation as he tugs my dress up to my hips. He presses a soft kiss against my lace-covered mound. I moan softly, the warmth of his breath teasing me through the delicate fabric.

Martin hooks his fingers into the waistband of my thong, slowly pulling it down. I kick off my heels, step out of my thong, and deliberately place one foot on the bed, opening myself up more for him. The fishnets accentuate every curve of my legs, and I'm glad I shaved for tonight—he has a close-up view of how turned on I am.

He licks his lips as he examines me. "You're gorgeous, Jessica."

I smile, running my fingers through his hair. "And you're talking too much." I gently push his head down, guiding him to where I want him.

"So eager," he murmurs against my inner thigh, just above where the fishnet ends.

The only thing I get out is, "You have no idea," before his mouth is on me–and oh god, his tongue. It's like velvet fire, exploring every sensitive spot. He's not just talented—he's fucking phenomenal. I gasp, my hips bucking against his mouth. He grips my ass, his fingers digging into the flesh, pulling me closer as he feasts on me like I'm his last meal.

He finds my clit, circling it with his tongue, applying just the right amount of pressure. My eyes close and my head falls back as pleasure crashes over me. "Fuck, Martin…" I moan, my fingers tightening in his hair. I'm loving every second of his skilled attention. His tongue traces intricate patterns, making me dizzy with delight. Each stroke is designed to drive me wild.

I'm a live wire, every nerve ending sparking with electricity. I can feel my orgasm building as the tension coils tighter and tighter. "Oh god, don't stop," I pant, grinding against his face.

He growls, the vibration sending me over the edge. I come hard and my body shakes. The tiny bell on my choker jingles with each tremor. My cries of pleasure fill the room, mingling with the delicate tinkling sound. He doesn't stop and rides out my orgasm with me. When I start coming down, his tongue gentles as the bell's chimes gradually slows with my movements.

As I catch my breath, I open my eyes to see him looking up at me. There's a satisfied smirk on his face. "You taste amazing."

I feel so good after the orgasm, all I can do is giggle, causing one last soft tinkle from my choker.

Fuck, Lucas outdid himself this time. I trace Martin's jaw with my fingers, feeling the slight stubble there. "Well, well, well, looks like you weren't exaggerating your skills. If I were rating you, you'd be a solid 10 out of 10. Your tongue deserves a fucking medal."

Martin chuckles and stands up, pulling me into a kiss. I can taste myself on him, and it's intoxicating. When I reach down to rub his cock, he stops me by seizing my wrists. "Not so fast, kitten. I was just the appetizer," he murmurs against my lips.

I pull back, surprised. "Appetizer? But I thought..."

He smiles. "Lucas has more planned for you tonight. You should text him."

Martin sets the keycard down on the nightstand, as if he's leaving it for me. Yeah, I need to find out what Lucas is up to. I'm still buzzing from my orgasm, but my curiosity is piqued. I grab my phone from my purse, and type out a quick message to Lucas.

Jessica: Just had the best appetizer with Martin. Any chance I can have the main course now? ;)

Lucas's response is almost immediate.

Lucas: Glad you enjoyed it, baby. There's plenty more where that came from. Want more guys tonight?

Mmm, nice. My fingers fly over the keyboard.

Jessica: After what Martin just did? I could fuck the entire party right now.

Lucas: That's my girl. Have fun, baby. I love you.

Before I can even put my phone down, there's a knock at the door. Oooh, shit. My heart races as I straighten my dress. I hustle over, and when I open it, Alex and Jordan are standing there, grinning. I recognize them instantly—more coworkers. We've met at company parties before, but I never imagined I'd fuck them. They're both tall, handsome, and looking at me like I'm their next meal.

Behind me, Martin slips out of the room. "Thanks for a great time, Jessica," he murmurs.

"You too, Martin." A thrill runs through me at how wonderfully slutty it is to be saying goodbye to one guy as two more join me. I turn to my new guests and give them a mischievous smile. "Well, hello there, boys. Welcome to the party."

My body tingles with anticipation. These familiar faces promise one hell of a night, especially in their costumes. Alex is decked out as a sexy cop, complete with a tight blue uniform and shiny badge. Jordan's robber outfit, with its black and white striped shirt and a pushed-up eye mask, adds a naughty contrast.

Alex's eyes devour me as they trail down to my fishnets. " Looks like we've got a sexy kitten to play with tonight," he drawls, his tone deep and rich. " And it seems she's been a very naughty girl."

Jordan lets out a low whistle. "Damn…Lucas mentioned your costume, but seeing is believing. You're hot. Those stockings are killing me."

Their attention makes me feel warm all over. I think back to our friendly chats at office gatherings, always dancing on the edge of flirtatious. I appreciate the compliments, but I need their cocks. NOW. I give them a coy look. "All talk and no action, boys? I thought you came here to play. Or is Officer Alex going to arrest me?"

Alex's eyebrow shoots up and a predatory grin spreads across his face. He stalks towards me, his fake handcuffs jingling at his hip. "Oh, we're here to play, kitten. But in this game, we make the rules. And rule number one?" He pauses, letting the tension build. "Good kittens get on their knees."

God, the way he says it. My body responds instantly. I blush and sink to my knees. Looking up, I can't resist teasing him a little. "And if I'm not a good kitten?"

Alex chuckles and grasps my chin, tilting my face up. "Then we'll have to teach you a lesson, won't we?" His thumb traces my lower lip, drawing out a soft moan. "But something tells me you'll be purring for us soon enough."

Jordan steps forward, his movements lazy but purposeful. The sound of his belt unbuckling makes me want to squirm. "Time to show us what that pretty mouth can do," he says in a husky tone. "We've got a special treat for our little kitten. Think you can handle a cop and a robber at once?"

"Mmm, I do love cream," I purr, watching Jordan pull his cock out and stroke himself. I'm enjoying this game. The playful humiliation only serves to turn me on more. "And I bet you two have been saving up a lot for me."

Alex follows suit, unzipping his pants and revealing his hard length. "If you're a good kitty, we'll give you plenty."

A rush of illicit delight runs through me at the thought of pleasing them, of being their good kitty. I want to give them as much pleasure as Martin just gave me. I take Alex's cock in my hand, stroking him gently before taking him into my mouth. He pulses against my tongue as I swirl it around his shaft. I love the power I have in this moment, the ability to make him moan with just my mouth and my hands.

Alex groans, his hand coming to rest on my head. "Fuck, that's good," he murmurs as he slides deeper into my mouth. I can feel the longing building within me with each swirl of my tongue. I'm not just doing this for them; I'm doing it for me, too. I love the taste of cocks and the feel of them.

I feel Jordan's hand on my chin, turning me towards him. I release Alex with a pop and give Jordan my attention, taking his cock into my mouth. He's just as hard, and I can taste the saltiness of his precum on my tongue. I love the contrast between them, the different tastes and textures, the different sounds they make. It's like a symphony of pleasure, and I'm the conductor.

I go back and forth between them, sucking and licking. My hands stroke whichever cock isn't in my mouth. Their moans fill the room. It spurs me on. I hear the tiny bell on my choker jingle with each movement. God, that's filthy. Their desire fuels my own. I love being a fucktoy.

Alex looks down at me with lust. "You're such a good kitten," he praises. His hand tightens in my hair, miraculously avoiding my cat ears. Pleasure rushes through me. I really do want to be their good kitty. Their naughty plaything. I want to make them lose control.

I moan around Jordan's cock. The vibrations make him groan. I'm lost in the moment as their hips move faster. They're close. I can't wait to feel their hot cream in my mouth—to taste their cum. I work harder, determined to be their good kitty. My body aches for pleasure, but I'm too focused on getting them off to care.

Alex's grip tightens in my hair. "Fuck, I'm close," he groans.

I look up at him. I want to watch him come. My eyes water as I take him deeper. My hand works with my mouth while my other hand is on Jordan.

"Me too, kitty," Jordan rasps. "Make us come."

I move my mouth to Jordan, sucking on him as hard as I can before switching to Alex again. The bell on my choker jingles softly as I alternate between them. This is so hot. I'm so close to making them both come—to giving them what they crave.

Alex comes first, his body shuddering as he groans, his cum filling my mouth. I swallow, enjoying the taste of his cum. He's yummy. I keep sucking until he's spent and his body relaxes.

I turn to Jordan, determined to make him come just as hard. I take him deep, my hand working the base of his shaft as my tongue swirls around him. He moans and his body jerks as he explodes, filling my mouth with his warm seed. I swallow as much as I can as some of it runs down my chin.

When I've milked all I can from both of them, I sit back and smile. My body thrums with satisfaction. I did it. I was their good kitty.

Speaking of being a kitty...I reach up to touch my cat ears, surprised to find them still in place. Huh, who knew these little ears could hold up through all that? Guess I'm just a perfect kitty.

A knock at the door makes me jump. What now?

CHAPTER 3

Alex and Jordan exchange a knowing glance. They know something I don't.

Alex tucks his cock into his pants, and I can't look away as he strolls to the door. My skin prickles with anticipation. He opens it, revealing two new faces. Oooh, more guys...for me? I examine my new playmates, and my mouth goes dry. One's dressed as a lumberjack, complete with a red plaid shirt and suspenders. The other's in a firefighter's uniform, minus the helmet. They're both tall and rugged, and they gaze at me with a thirst that ignites a tingling heat across my skin.

The lumberjack speaks. "Lucas sent us. He said to find Jessica and fuck her hard."

My heart squeezes with joy. Lucas arranged this. For me. For us. I eye the two new guys as I imagine them both inside me. I'd love to be the meat in that sandwich.

I tease Alex. "You going to let them in?"

Alex steps aside, ushering them in. The air crackles with electricity as they enter, and my body hums with anticipation. I can't wait to feel their cocks inside me.

Alex returns to me, bending down for a quick kiss. Jordan does the same, his lips pressing against mine more insistently. The contrast in their kisses makes my stomach flutter from desire.

"It's time for your main course," Jordan jokes, his eyes twinkling with mischief.

Alex grins. "Yeah, you're in for a treat, kitten."

As Alex and Jordan slip out, the door clicks shut behind them. The room feels charged with possibility. I'm hyper-aware of every sensation as my skin tingling. All this attention makes me feel more alive than ever.

The lumberjack steps forward, his presence commanding the room. He's muscular, with piercing green eyes and blonde hair. A well-groomed beard frames his strong jaw, adding to his rugged appeal. "I'm Gabe," he says, his deep voice sending a shiver down my spine. He gestures to his companion. "This is Sam."

The firefighter, Sam, is equally impressive. Dark hair and a muscular frame. Both men appear to be in their late 30s, exuding a mature confidence that makes my pulse quicken.

I stand, legs shaky. Gabe follows my every move, while Sam's gaze lingers on my curves. I feel exhilarated, and I take a step towards them as if drawn by an irresistible force.

Gabe's eyes roam over my body, pausing at my stockings. "Lucas told us you like it rough. Is that true?"

A rush of heat hits me as I answer, "Yes." Oh yeah, Lucas is going to have one happy kitten when he gets home.

Sam steps closer, his uniform rustling. "Good, because we're going to fuck you hard. And Lucas wants you to record it on your phone."

Oooh, nice. The thought of recording this is kinky and naughty—I love it. I dig through my purse, and my fingers tremble as I grab my phone. Setting it up on the dresser, I make sure it's just right. Can't miss a thing.

Sam moves in close. His warm hands slide up my legs, caressing my stockings. He pushes my dress higher, then lifts it off, tossing it aside. The intensity of the moment makes me tremble.

Gabe unhooks my strapless bra with practiced ease, his lumberjack shirt brushing against my skin. The bra falls away, leaving me naked except for the choker with its tiny bell and my stockings. My nipples harden in the cool air. For a moment, I feel exposed, vulnerable. But then I catch Gabe's hungry gaze, and I push aside my hesitation and embrace the moment.

His hand finds its way between my legs. I gasp at his touch as he murmurs appreciatively, "You're so wet."

"Yes," I moan, arching my back. "I'm ready. Please…"

For a moment, time seems to slow down. I think about how wonderful Lucas is for arranging this. I'm glad I'm recording this for him.

Sam's voice cuts through my thoughts. "Get on the bed. On all fours like a good kitten."

Mmm, hell yes. I comply, crawling onto the bed at an angle that gives the camera a side view of the action. I feel Gabe position himself behind me, his hand stroking my ass gently at first. "You've been a naughty kitten, haven't you?" His palm comes down hard on my ass as pings of pleasure light up my brain.

What? I've been a good kitten. But the sensation feels so good, I don't complain. Each spank sinks me into a deeper state of submission. I want to please him, to show him I can be good.

"Tell me you want this," he growls, spanking me again, harder this time. I feel the heat rise across my skin. I didn't expect to get spanked tonight, but I'm loving this.

"I need it," I whimper, my body already aching for him. The sting of his hand mixes with the warmth spreading through me, and I feel the world going fuzzy from pleasure.

"Beg for it, Jessica," he commands. "Beg for my cock like a filthy slut."

"Please, can I have your cock? Please? I've been a good kitten," I plead. I can hear the neediness in my tone, but I don't care. I just want his cock.

My mind is a haze of pleasure, every fiber of my being yearning to please him. He grasps my hips, his cock pressing against my entrance briefly before he thrusts straight to my core. I squeal when he bottoms out and presses against my ass. Holy fuck, he's huge. This is probably why Lucas chose him—though god knows how Lucas seems to know if a guy has a large cock or not. This is something I don't question and just enjoy the men he chooses for me.

"Fuck, you're tight," he groans. He's so thick there's a mixture of pleasure and delicious pain as I stretch to accommodate him. When he pulls out all the way and then slams into me, I moan in bliss as my body responds to his roughness. He sets a steady rhythm, and my mind whirls from the delight.

I barely notice when Sam kneels on the bed in front of me until his cock is at my lips. There's a bead of pre-cum glistening at the tip. I lick my lips as my mouth waters at the sight of him. I can already imagine the feel of him on my tongue, the taste of his precum filling my mouth. His cock is large as well, though I would guess not as big as the monster in my pussy. It's thick and veined, the tip swollen and an angry red, just begging to be sucked.

He fists my hair, pulling me up to look at him and somehow not dislodging my cat ears. His eyes shimmer with lust. "Look at it," he growls. "See how much I want you? Now, be a good kitten and suck me."

Mmm, I'll be the best kitten there is if they keep up the dirty talk. I wrap my lips around the head, inhaling his musky scent, and run my tongue over the tip, gathering that salty sweetness.

He groans, his grip on my hair tightening. "Fuck," he grunts. "You're such a good fucktoy. Show me how much you want it."

I open my mouth wider, taking him in inch by inch. I swirl my tongue along his shaft, feeling every ridge and vein.

Pleasure swirls in my core, my own desire growing as I deep throat him. I love giving blow jobs, the power it gives me to bring a strong man to his knees. He might be using me for his pleasure, but I'm really the one in control because I'm letting him.

When Gabe pulls out of my pussy and drills back in repeatedly, all thoughts fly from my mind. I'm going to come hard, I can tell.

The room fills with our moans and the slap of flesh against flesh. Our sounds delight me. The bell at my neck tinkles with each movement, a delicate counterpoint to our primal sounds. I can feel the tension increasing, promising an explosive climax. The bell chimes faster, matching our frenzied pace.

"You like that, don't you?" Sam says, his voice filled with lust. "You like being fucked by two men at once, being used for our pleasure."

A rush of longing ripples through me, and I moan around his cock, the vibrations making him groan. Yes, I love it. I love the feel of them, the taste of them, the sounds they make when they're inside me. I enjoy being the center of attention, and I love the way they use me, the way they make me feel alive.

Gabe's thrusts become more urgent. "Fuck, your pussy is so tight, so wet," he groans. "I'm going to fill you so full of cum it will be dripping out of you all the way home."

Oh god, it probably will. The thought of going home with a pussy full of another man's cum is the filthy payoff from doing this. I love how much of a slut I feel like after I take loads of cum that aren't my husband's.

Gabe's hand moves to my clit, rubbing it in quick circles. "Is the slut going to come for us?"

I moan out, "Yes," but it's muffled by Sam's cock in my mouth as Gabe continues.

"Let me feel your pussy clench around my cock, and I'll fill this pretty little pussy full of cum."

His words are like a match to gasoline, igniting a fire within me that threatens to consume me whole. The sensation is overwhelming, every thrust sending shockwaves of pleasure through me. My thighs quiver, and my body tightens.

Gabe's thrusts become erratic. "Fuck, I'm going to come," he groans, his body tensing behind me.

The thought of his cum dripping out of me is enough to skyrocket me over the edge. Sam pulls out of my mouth, and I scream in pleasure, my body convulsing as I come hard. Rapture sizzles my brain as my pussy clenches around Gabe's cock, forcing him to come.

Gabe grunts and stills as his warm cum coats my inner walls. I rock against him, milking his cock for every last drop as pleasure ripples from my fingertips to my toes.

When Gabe's done unloading, he pulls out. Sam immediately flips me onto my back, spreading my legs wide. He kneels between them, his cock glistening with my saliva.

"I want to see your face when you come again," he says. "I want to watch you fall apart."

He thrusts into me, hard and deep, making me gasp in delight. His movements are fast and urgent, and he's hitting a wonderful spot with each whack against my pussy. He leans down, his mouth capturing mine in a rough, passionate kiss.

"You're so fucking hot," he murmurs against my lips. "I can't get enough of you. I want to fuck you all night, make you come over and over again."

Mmm, sounds good to me. I wrap my legs around him, pulling him deeper, meeting his thrusts with my own. The sensation of his cock filling me is overwhelming.

"Fuck me harder," I moan. "Make me come again."

His hips move in a relentless rhythm, each thrust spiraling me closer to the peak. When his hand snakes down, finding my clit and rubbing it in tight circles, I can't hold back any longer. I scream, my body spasming as white lights burst along the corners of my vision from pleasure, leaving me shaking.

Sam groans loudly, his body jerking as he fills me full of hot cum. I can feel every pulse of his release, the warmth spreading inside me, making me clench around him. He collapses on top of me, both of us panting. The warmth of his seed mixing with

Gabe's is filthy, and I squeeze my muscles around him, savoring the sensation of having so much cum inside me.

A ripple of pleasure makes me giggle. Goddamn, if I don't have the best husband in the world. This night has been everything I wanted and more. I'm thrilled and I'm used, and I loved every second of it.

We all take a moment to catch our breaths before the guys start getting dressed. The atmosphere is light and playful, and they joke with me about how this will make the company parties more interesting as they remember tonight. God yes, I just played with five of my husband's coworkers. Company parties are going to make me blush like crazy. When Ms. Kitty buzzes in pleasure, I hold in a giggle. Yeah, we're going to like the slight humiliation.

My body still tingles with the remnants of pleasure. I gather my clothes, slipping into my cat costume. The costume that felt playful and sexy now feels like a symbol of my slutty night's adventures. I'll walk through the lobby looking like I was just fucked hard, and I don't care. I'm going to own it.

I turn the camera off, and I shiver with pleasure at the thought of Lucas's reaction. He's going to be crazed for me after watching the video. I can't wait to share this experience with him.

We leave the hotel room together, and with a final goodbye in the lobby, I strut to reception to check out. The woman takes one look at me and doesn't question whether everything was all right with the room since I'm leaving without staying the full night. Yeah...she knows what's up.

As I make my way out to my car, the cool night air hits my face, bringing me back to reality. The drive home is a blur, my mind filled with memories of the night.

As soon as I'm home, I make a beeline for the shower, letting the hot water wash over me, cleansing my body but not the memories. I can still feel their hands on me, their bodies against mine, the pleasure they gave me. It's a feeling I want to hold onto, to savor.

After my shower, I wrap myself in a soft towel and make my way to the bedroom. I pick up my phone, attaching the video to a simple message for Lucas.

Jessica: Can't wait to see you tomorrow, love. Here's the video for you.

I climb into bed naked and sigh in happiness. I'm exhausted, but my mind is racing with thoughts of Lucas, of what he'll think, of what he'll do when he sees the video. I'd be surprised if he doesn't jack off while watching it. I bet it's hot.

As I drift off to sleep, I feel a sense of contentment. This night has been a wild ride, and I can't wait to see Lucas. Tomorrow is going to be one hell of a day.

CHAPTER 4

The next morning, I stir, the warmth of Lucas's body pressed against mine seeping into my consciousness. A smile tugs at my lips as I snuggle closer. My body is still humming with memories of last night.

Suddenly, Lucas's grip tightens as he leans over me, and my heart flutters as I look at him. His hazel eyes smolder with barely contained passion and something else—a raw, primal intensity that makes my skin prickle.

"Good morning, baby," he murmurs, and the lust in his tone resonates deep within me.

The sheets slide down, and my pulse races with anticipation when I realize he's naked. "Morning, love. When did you get home?"

He doesn't answer right away, his gaze locked on mine, making my breath hitch. He parts my legs and pins me to the bed with his body. I moan as I feel his cock against my pussy. He's rubbing the length of himself against my folds, and the friction against my clit is a pleasurable sensation.

"I just got home. I watched the video last night," he says, his voice filled with a mix of desire and possessiveness that makes my pulse race. "You were incredible. So fucking hot."

A thrill runs through me, and I moan, "I knew you'd like it."

He captures my lips in a rough, passionate kiss. "I loved it," he growls against my mouth. "Seeing you like that, with those men...it drove me wild."

I rock against him, moaning each time he slides against my clit. "Show me. Show me how wild it made you."

He groans and repositions himself before entering me with a single, hard thrust. I gasp from pleasure and wrap my legs around him as he starts fucking me. He's not gentle, not slow—he's almost feral, and I love it.

"You're mine," he growls. Every word is punctuated by a thrust that drives me higher. "Mine to fuck, mine to pleasure. Mine to share and mine to take back."

I'm arching my back, meeting his thrusts with my own, feeling the pleasure build. "Yes," I gasp. "I'm yours. Always yours."

He thrusts harder, each movement sending jolts of bliss through me. It's intoxicating, and I can't get enough of it.

"You liked being fucked by them, didn't you?" His eyes lock onto mine, seeing right through me. "You liked being used by guys I chose, knowing I was going to watch it later and do this."

"Yes," I moan, my body trembling with pleasure. "I loved every second of it. But I love this more. I love you more."

He groans as if my words are too much for him, and he shudders as he comes. The sensation of him filling me pushes me over the edge, and I explode with pleasure as I cry out. He fucks me through my orgasm, and I'm still trembling when he pulls out and collapses on the bed next to me. God, what a way to wake up.

Lucas pulls me into his arms, his grip tight, possessive, and I feel safe, cherished. "I love you," he murmurs. "You're mine, always mine."

I smile as a warmth of love fills my belly. "I love you too. Always and forever."

As we lie there, our bodies entwined, I can't help but giggle. "You know, this is the second Halloween in a row you've surprised me. You're setting quite the precedent here."

Lucas's chest rumbles with laughter. "Is that so, baby?" His fingers trace lazy circles on my skin. "Well, I'm up for the challenge. I'll have to think of something really good for next year."

I snuggle closer, feeling Ms. Kitty purr contentedly. "Mmm, I can't wait. You spoil me."

"You deserve it," he murmurs, kissing the top of my head. "Besides, I got to watch the video. That was the hottest thing I've ever seen and a gift that will keep on giving."

A zing of pleasure ripples through me at the thought of him watching it again. Maybe I'll get him to watch it with me one night. The kitten in me is very curious about what other surprises my sexy, thoughtful husband has in store for us, but one thing's for certain—our love story is only getting hotter with each passing chapter.

The End

Join my newsletter for some ebook bonus stories with Jessica. Find them on my website at:
https://www.lacey-cross.net/cabinadventure

WANT MORE OF JESSICA?

I have 7 other stories with Jessica. Start with the bundle that includes her first-time experience.

5 filthy hotwife stories. A slutty wife, a loving husband, and oh-so-many men.

My husband has a dirty desire to share me and listen in. When I agreed to it, I didn't realize how much I'd love being spread wide, pounded hard, and used in so many filthy ways.

Includes:

Sharing his Adventurous Wife

He has a desire to share his wife. She's not so sure she needs it... until he stages an entire weekend designed to lead her into the hotwife lifestyle.

Sharing Her Treats

When her husband wins haunted house tickets in a raffle, she didn't know it included a rough pounding.

Sharing His Eager Hotwife

A loving husband gets off on choosing the men to use his hotwife.

Shared Hotwife at the Con

Jessica has a fantasy of getting a rough pounding from a massive, beefcake of a man. A chance encounter at a con fulfills her filthy dreams as she gets used roughly and filled.

Sharing His Gift Twice

She thought her husband forgot it was Valentine's Day. Instead, he thrills her with a filthy gift.

These stories contain graphic depictions of sex between consenting adults and features elements of hotwife, and multiple men. Reader discretion advised.

Find it at your favorite retailer.

About Lacey Cross

Lacey Cross is a wife-sharing erotica writer with over 100 short stories published since she started in 2021. Her stories emphasize the pleasure found from the wife living her best slut life and embracing the hotwife lifestyle. She explores themes of free use, submissive wives with dominant bulls, BDSM… and oh-so-many men.

Find her books, erotic shorts, and audiobooks on her website: https://lacey-cross.com/

If you like romantic BDSM erotica, check out her April Cross books at:

https://april-cross.com/

www.ingramcontent.com/pod-product-compliance
Lightning Source LLC
Chambersburg PA
CBHW031555310726
48973CB00003B/828